Legally Hilarious

Melissa Palmer

 pencil

ISBN 978-93-5883-082-8
© Melissa Palmer 2023

Published in India 2023 by Pencil

A brand of
One Point Six Technologies Pvt. Ltd.
Unit no. 26, Ground Floor, Building A1,
Wadala Truck Terminal Road,
Near Post Office, Antop Hill, Mumbai - 400037
E connect@thepencilapp.com
W www.thepencilapp.com

Author biography

About The Author:

Melissa Palmer lives in the mountains of Western North Carolina. She is a mother, wife secretary, homeschool instructor, ongoing college student, an author, and she runs Moving Mountains Recovery Hotline, a telephone and resource service for addicts in recovery. Melissa is an addict in recovery for 11 years and counting. Though her passion is both reading books and writing them, she enjoys helping people as well. Melissa is very passionate about her career and very determined to accomplish her goals as she continues down this path of creative writing and education.

CONTENTS

Prologue

"Legally Hilarious" is a comedy novel that takes readers on a hilarious journey through the lives of lawyers who dared to reveal the lighter side of the legal world. With its witty dialogue, absurd situations, and unforgettable characters, this book promises to leave readers in stitches while shedding light on the often overlooked comedic moments in the courtroom.

"There's No Rest For the Wicked or Those Who Defend Them"
Attorney Tony Dalton

Ch.1 The Courtroom Chronicles

In the bustling city of Verdict Ville, a group of lawyers had a secret. They were tired of the serious and often monotonous nature of their profession. They decided to let loose and reveal the comical side of their lives in a tell-all book. The lawyers, each with their unique quirks and eccentricities, were ready to share their hilarious stories with the world. Meet Sarah Summers, a brilliant attorney known for her sharp wit and impeccable fashion sense. She was the first to propose the idea of writing a book that would expose the absurdity of the legal world. Sarah was determined to highlight the humorous situations, embarrassing mishaps, and outrageous characters that crossed their paths every day. Sarah was a diligent lawyer who had built up a reputation amongst her peers for her dogged dedication to the case in hand. She had represented countless clients over the years, but this particular case was by far the most challenging she had ever faced. The defendant was a notorious criminal, a man who had been accused of a series of brutal murders that had shocked the local community. He had been given one chance at redemption, and if he failed, he faced certain death at the hands of the state. The prosecution team was led by the skilled Mr. Tanner, a man who had been instrumental in securing countless convictions over the years. Sarah's job was to prove that the defendant was innocent, and if she could do so, his life would be spared. The trial began, and Sarah was on the stand, facing challenging questions from the judge and the jury. She focused on the facts of the case, presenting evidence that supported her argument that the defendant was not responsible for the murders. As the trial progressed, the defendant continued to maintain his innocence. His family members claimed he was a changed man, remorseful for his past sins, but the jury didn't believe it. They found him guilty of all charges and handed down the death sentence. The sentencing phase of the trial was intense. Sarah had to appeal to the jury, trying to make them see the defendant's life in a different light. She put forward a compelling argument, begging them to show mercy and spare his life, but it was to no avail. The next morning, Sarah's phone rang, and she was surprised to hear the voice of the defendant on the other line. He had asked to speak to her privately, and she agreed to meet him in a nearby coffee shop. As she sat down with him, his face showed no emotion. He simply told her that he was innocent. He admitted to killing the people in the house, but he didn't commit the other murders. He had been framed by someone powerful, someone with a vested interest in seeing him condemned. Sarah was shocked. She couldn't believe what she was hearing. She went to the police and filed a report. The investigation was launched, and soon enough, evidence began to point to a rival criminal gang who had framed the defendant to cover up their own crimes. The case was overturned, and the real culprits were brought to justice. The defendant was released from prison, and he walked out a free man. Years later, Sarah looked back on that case with mixed feelings. Although she had accomplished what she set out to do, she knew that the process had cost her a lot. She had been subjected to a relentless media scrutiny, her personal life had been torn apart, and she had even lost some of her friends and colleagues as a result of the public's obsession with the case. But she also felt a sense of vindication. She had proven that the defendant was innocent, even if it took a second trial and a lot of hard work. She knew that it was worth it, that it was the right thing to do. And so, as she sat in her private practice, surrounded by the faces of her clients, she felt a sense of peace. For her, the case was finally resolved, and she could focus on the present and the future.

Ch. 2 The Law Firm Circus

Sarah's law firm, Summers & Associates, was a hotbed of comedy. From the outrageous office pranks to the never-ending battle for the best parking spot, the lawyers had developed a unique camaraderie that kept them sane amidst the chaos. In this chapter, readers would be introduced to the firm's partners, including the always-stressed Mr. Henderson, the clumsy but well-meaning Mr. Johnson, and the eccentric Ms. Smith, who had a peculiar obsession with collecting gavels. In this chapter, join Mr. Henderson on his journey to find comic relief amidst the pressures of his legal professionMr. Henderson, a middle-aged attorney, was known for his exceptional legal skills and unwavering dedication to his clients. However, his relentless pursuit of justice often left him stressed and in desperate need of some comic relief. Amidst the serious nature of his profession, Mr. Henderson sought to find humor in the most unexpected places. One day, Mr. Henderson found himself assigned to work closely with a new colleague, Mr. Jenkins, who was notorious for his eccentric behavior. With an unruly mop of hair, mismatched socks, and an infectious laugh, Mr. Jenkins seemed to possess an endless supply of comical anecdotes. Mr. Henderson couldn't help but be amused by his colleague's unconventional approach to life.During a high-profile trial, Mr. Henderson found himself in a tense courtroom battle. As the opposing attorney presented his case, a series of unexpected mishaps began to occur. From a squeaky chair causing uncontrollable laughter to a rogue pigeon flying through the courtroom, chaos ensued. Mr. Henderson's stress momentarily vanished as he, along with the judge and jury, burst into fits of laughter. Mr. Henderson's next case involved a peculiar client, Mrs. Griswold, who had a penchant for outrageous conspiracy theories. Despite the seriousness of her legal predicament, Mrs. Griswold's outlandish tales provided Mr. Henderson with endless entertainment. From her belief in a secret society of alien garden gnomes to her insistence that her neighbor's cat was a government spy, Mr. Henderson couldn't help but chuckle at her imaginative stories. In an attempt to alleviate the constant stress, Mr. Henderson and his colleagues engaged in a series of office pranks. From filling the water cooler with grape juice to swapping staplers with rubber ducks, the attorneys found solace in their mischievous antics. These lighthearted moments brought much-needed laughter and camaraderie to an otherwise intense workplace. During one particular trial, Mr. Henderson encountered a courtroom sketch artist with a knack for caricatures. As the artist captured the essence of each person in the courtroom, his exaggerated drawings brought smiles to everyone's faces. Mr. Henderson couldn't help but admire the artist's ability to find humor in the most serious of situations. In an attempt to bring some much-needed fun to the office, Mr. Henderson organized an unforgettable office party. From karaoke competitions to a comedy roast of their boss, the attorneys let loose and enjoyed a night filled with laughter and merriment. The party served as a reminder that even in the midst of stress, there was always room for joy. During a routine court appearance, Mr. Henderson found himself involved in a hilarious mix-up. Due to a clerical error, he was mistaken for a comedian scheduled to perform at a nearby theater. Instead of arguing, Mr. Henderson decided to embrace the situation and delivered an impromptu stand-up comedy routine that left the courtroom in stitches. As Mr. Henderson continued to seek comical relief in his daily life, he realized that laughter was not just a temporary escape from stress, but a powerful tool for resilience and connection. By infusing humor into his professional and personal life, Mr. Henderson not only found joy but also inspired those around him to find laughter in the most unexpected places.. With eccentric colleagues, bizarre courtroom incidents, and hilarious client encounters, Mr. Henderson discovers that laughter truly is the best medicine. Through his hilarious adventures, Mr. Henderson not only learns to cope with stress but also reminds us all of the importance of finding humor in our everyday lives. Mr. Johnson was an attorney known for his impeccable work ethic and his unwavering dedication to justice. However, he was also known for being incredibly clumsy. No matter how hard he tried, he seemed to find himself in the most absurd and comical situations. One sunny morning, Mr. Johnson woke up with a smile on his face, determined to make the most of his day. Little did he know that fate had a series of mishaps planned for him. As he rushed to the bathroom, he tripped over his own shoelaces and crashed into the door, knocking it off its hinges.With a sheepish grin, he muttered to himself, "Looks like it's going to be one of those days." But Mr. Johnson refused to let his clumsiness dampen his spirits. He quickly fixed the door and proceeded to get ready for work. As he walked down the street, his briefcase in hand, he couldn't help but notice a stray dog following him. Feeling a pang of sympathy, he decided to take the dog to the local animal shelter. However, as he attempted to pick up the dog, he accidentally stepped on its tail, causing it to yelp in pain. Embarrassed and apologetic, Mr. Johnson tried to calm the dog down, but his clumsiness seemed to follow him everywhere. He stumbled over his own feet and ended up falling into a nearby fountain, soaking himself from head to toe. Passersby couldn't help but burst into laughter at the sight of the drenched attorney. Arriving at his office dripping wet, Mr. Johnson was greeted with a chorus of laughter from his colleagues. Despite the humiliation, he couldn't help but join in, realizing that his clumsiness brought a much-needed dose of comedy to their otherwise serious workplace. Throughout the day, Mr. Johnson's clumsiness continued to provide moments of hilarity. He accidentally spilled coffee on important documents, mistook a potted plant for a colleague, and even managed to trip over his own chair during a meeting. Despite the chaos, his big heart and genuine concern for others never wavered. One day, as Mr. Johnson was leaving the courthouse after a particularly eventful trial, he bumped into a woman named Emily. Emily, a quirky and free-spirited artist, had a contagious laughter that instantly caught Mr. Johnson's attention. They struck up a conversation, and to his surprise, Emily found his clumsiness endearing. As their friendship blossomed, Mr. Johnson found a new lease on life. Emily introduced him to the world of comedy clubs and improv shows, where he could embrace his clumsiness and turn it into something hilarious. He started attending comedy classes and even performed stand-up routines, much to the delight of the audience. With Emily's support, Mr. Johnson discovered that laughter truly was the best medicine. His newfound confidence and ability to laugh at himself transformed his life and career. He became known as the attorney with a big heart and an infectious sense of humor. Together, Mr. Johnson and Emily navigated the ups and downs of life, always finding humor in the most unexpected places. Their love story was filled with laughter, mishaps, and a deep appreciation for the joy that comedy brought to their lives. In the end, Mr. Johnson realized that his clumsiness was not a curse but a blessing. It had led him to find true love and a new purpose in life. And so, he continued to stumble through each day, embracing the comedy that seemed to follow him wherever he went, knowing that it was an essential part of who he was. Ms. Smith, a middle-aged attorney with a peculiar obsession for collecting gavels, was known for her vibrant personality and unorthodox approach to the legal profession. Her office resembled a museum of gavels, each one meticulously arranged on shelves, desks, and even hanging from the ceiling. The collection had grown so vast that it was rumored to rival that of the most prestigious auction houses. One sunny morning, Ms. Smith found herself embroiled in a peculiar courtroom conundrum. She was representing Mr. Thompson, a man accused of stealing a rare, antique gavel from a local historical society. The irony of the situation was not lost on Ms. Smith, who secretly admired the audacity of such a theft. As the trial began, Ms. Smith entered the courtroom with a confident stride, her collection of gavels hidden beneath her black robe. The judge, unaware of her obsession, eyed her curiously but said nothing. The prosecution presented its evidence, including security camera footage that clearly showed Mr. Thompson pocketing the gavel. Ms. Smith, known for her quick wit and sharp tongue, rose to her feet. With a mischievous glint in her eye, she began her cross-examination. As she fired questions at the prosecution's witnesses, she subtly tapped a small gavel hidden in her hand, causing a ripple of amusement among the courtroom spectators. During a recess, Ms. Smith retreated to her office, surrounded by her beloved gavels. She meticulously examined each one, searching for a hidden clue that could turn the tide in Mr. Thompson's favor. Her collection had become more than just a hobby; it was now her secret weapon.Inspiration struck as Ms. Smith discovered an old, weathered gavel with a hidden compartment. Inside, she found a faded document that revealed the true origins of the stolen antique gavel. It turned out that the gavel had been donated by Mr. Thompson's grandfather, making it a family heirloom. Back in the courtroom, Ms. Smith unveiled her newfound evidence, stunning the prosecution and leaving the judge in awe. The courtroom erupted in laughter as Ms. Smith presented the document, her gavel collection serving as a backdrop to the spectacle. The judge, unable to contain his amusement, declared a mistrial, much to the dismay of the prosecution. Ms. Smith had single-handedly turned the tables, proving Mr. Thompson's innocence and exposing the true value of the stolen gavel. Word of Ms. Smith's courtroom theatrics spread like wildfire, attracting media attention from around the world. News outlets hailed her as the "Gavel Galore," and her collection became the talk of the town. Ms. Smith's quirky obsession with gavels took on a new dimension as she embraced her newfound fame. She opened a museum dedicated to gavels and their historical significance, inviting visitors to explore her vast collection. The museum became a popular tourist attraction, drawing crowds from far and wide. Ms. Smith's legacy as the Gavel Galore continued long after her retirement from the legal profession. Her collection became a symbol of her unique approach to life, reminding people to embrace their passions, no matter how peculiar they may be. As for Mr. Thompson, he went on to become a respected historian, dedicated to preserving the stories behind the gavels that had once adorned Ms. Smith's office. The stolen antique gavel found its rightful place in the historical society, serving as a reminder of the power of justice and the unpredictable turns of fate. And so, the story of Ms. Smith, the attorney with a peculiar obsession for collecting gavels, came to a close, leaving behind a legacy of laughter, wit, and the enduring pursuit of one's passions. Sarah's eyes skimmed the list of appointments printed on the board behind her. She was running behind and was exhausted from the week she had just had. She worked hard and long hours every day to keep the office running smoothly, and today was no exception. She sighed and rubbed her temples. She couldn't believe how time flew when she was busy. She was thankful that today she had no appointments scheduled, but she knew that wouldn't last long. She needed to prepare for the next case, which was already on her desk waiting for her attention.Sarah walked to her office, made some coffee, and settled in her chair. She took a sip of her coffee and contemplated the next case. It was a difficult one, she knew, but it wouldn't be easy to defend the plaintiff's side in this case. She had been hired by the defendant to represent him, but she had her doubts. The defendant was a wealthy man, and he had been accused of stealing from his own company. The plaintiff was a low-wage employee who had been laid off due to a merge, and she was now suing the defendant for wrongful dismissal. Sarah was conflicted about taking the case. She had always believed in the rule of law, but this case felt wrong to her. Her doubts didn't last long. A phone rang in her office, and she quickly grabbed it. It was her secretary."Hello, Sarah. It's Miss Johnson," her secretary said in a hurried tone."Hello, Miss Johnson. What can I do for you?" Sarah asked."Well, there's a gentleman here who is suing our company for wrongful dismissal. He's not a high-paying client, but he's very passionate about the matter. I thought you ought to know," Miss Johnson said, not wasting any time.Sarah nodded, wondering who this gentleman could be. "Thank you, Miss Johnson. Is there anything else?""Oh, no, that's it. But I thought I might give you a heads-up as to what's coming your way. Do you have time for a cup of coffee with me?" Miss Johnson asked.Sarah smiled, thinking she might as well take the chance. "Sure, why not?" Miss Johnson accompanied Sarah to the coffee shop in the next building, where Sarah ordered a latte. She was glad she had taken Miss Johnson up on her invitation, as the coffee was delicious. Miss Johnson took another sip and looked at Sarah over the rim of her cup. "So, what's on your mind?" Sarah took a deep breath, knowing she needed to confide in someone. "I have a case that I'm conflicted about taking. The plaintiff is upset over her dismissal, and the defendant is a wealthy man. I don't know if it's right to represent him." Miss Johnson looked at her, her eyes wide open. "You're kidding me. You're not sure if it's right to represent him?" Sarah shook her head. "No, I'm not. I know I was hired to represent him, but I can't ignore my moral compass." Miss Johnson leaned in, her voice low. "It's okay to have doubts, Sarah. You're a lawyer, not a robot. However, I can't stress enough how important it is to stand up for what's right. Sometimes, we need to take a stand even if it's not easy." Sarah nodded. "I know. Do you have any advice?" Miss Johnson smiled, thinking she knew just the thing. "I have a friend who has been through some tough times, and she swore by this. She said that you should take a piece of paper and write down all your doubts and walk out of your office, and not look back until you're sure that you did the right thing." Sarah smiled. "That's brilliant." Miss Johnson proceeded to give Sarah a list of contacts who could offer her advice and resources. Sarah thanked her and promised to take the case under consideration. She was still unsure of what to do, but she knew that she wouldn't make a decision until she had all the information. The next few days, Sarah pored over the case files, reading everything she could about the plaintiff's side and the defendant's side. She talked to her clients, the legal team, and even the judge. She learned about everything from the glaring mistakes the defendant had made in his company to the hurtful comments the plaintiff had made. While there was no doubt that the defendant was at fault, the plaintiff's side was just as convincing. The defendant had treated the plaintiff unfairly and had lost her job due to the company's financial crisis. The plaintiff was now unemployed, with no other options. In the end, Sarah decided to represent the defendant. She felt sympathetic towards him, but she knew that he had made a mistake. She also knew that he was an intelligent man who had a smart lawyer like her defending him. She reminded herself that she was a lawyer, not a judge. She had to weigh the evidence and make a decision based on the law. She promised herself that she would stand up for what was right, and she would never compromise her values as a lawyer again.Months passed, and Sarah was back in her office, with a smile on her face. She looked around and noticed how different her office was now. There were no more piles of files, and no more deadlines to keep up with.She took another sip of her coffee and smiled, thinking about how things had turned out. She had defended the defendant, and he had been found guilty. While it was a difficult time, she knew that it was a victory for justice.She looked out of her window and noticed the sun beginning to set. It was already late, and she knew that she had to get ready for a dinner with some friends. She quickly cleaned up her desk, making sure that everything was in order.As she made her way out of her office, she couldn't help but feel happy. She realized that there were lots of things that could make her happy, but being a good lawyer was one of them. As she walked down the hallway, she saw Miss Johnson, who had been her secretary for years."Hello, Sarah. How are you?" Miss Johnson asked, standing up from her desk. "I'm good, thanks. I just finished a dinner, and I have to go home now," Sarah said, smiling. Miss Johnson nodded, knowing that Sarah would need to go home soon. "Well, goodnight, Sarah. Have a good night." Sarah smiled, knowing that she would. She had learned a lot from her case, and she knew that it had changed her views. She was no longer in the business of getting the verdict that was right, but instead, she was in the business of doing what was right. As she walked out of the building, she felt happy to know that she had found herself in a profession that she could be proud of. She had worked hard and long, but it had all paid off. She had become a lawyer who was guided by her moral compass, just like Miss Johnson had suggested.

Ch.3 The Case of the Missing Pants

One day, a strange case landed on Sarah's desk. A client named Mr. Thompson had sued a dry cleaner for losing his favorite pants. What seemed like a simple case turned into a hilarious series of events. Sarah and her colleagues embarked on a journey to uncover the truth behind the mysteriously vanished trousers. Along the way, they encountered quirky witnesses, including a parrot who claimed to have seen the pants walking out of the store. Mr. Thompson sat in his office, feeling frustrated. The morning had started out well, but now he couldn't seem to find his son's missing pants. He had taken his son to the store this morning, and while his son was playing in the store, he had gone to the bathroom. When he returned, his son's pants were nowhere to be found.Mr. Thompson's son was a typical eight year old boy. He loved playing outside, and he often misliked his clothes. Mr. Thompson often had to help him put them on and help him keep them on. That's why the missing pants were so important. He needed them to be able to take him outside for recess.After searching the house and outside, Mr. Thompson had given up. He called the store's customer service line and asked if anyone had reported a lost item. The customer service representative told him that there was no record of a missing item. As Mr. Thompson hung up the phone, he heard a pop from the back room. His son's missing pants had been found. The pants were sitting on the counter, right where he had left them. Mr. Thompson's son was overjoyed. He hugged Mr. Thompson and thanked him for finding his missing pants. Mr. Thompson smiled, realizing that sometimes it's better to be lucky than to be prepared. The missing pants turned out to be a blessing in disguise. When his son went outside, he and his friends were able to play in the sun for hours, without worrying about whether or not they had all their clothes on.Mr. Thompson decided that he would make sure that his son never lost anything again. He went to the store and purchased a waterproof bag for him to keep his belongings in. From that day forward, Mr. Thompson made it a priority to always keep a bag or bin of some kind on hand, so that his son wouldn't have to worry about their contents ever disappearing again. As for the missing pants, Mr. Thompson never forgot the strange incident and always carried a waterproof bag with him, just in case. He had learned that sometimes, the unexpected can be a blessing, and that it pays to be prepared.

Ch.4 The Courtroom Catastrophes

As the lawyers delved deeper into their legal adventures, they found themselves in absurd courtroom situations. From a judge who mistook a gavel for a microphone to a witness who couldn't stop sneezing during cross-examination, the courtroom became a stage for comedic mishaps. Sarah and her colleagues struggled to maintain their professionalism while stifling their laughter. In the bustling city of Jesterfield, a group of lawyers gathered every Friday night at a local bar called "Legally Intoxicated." They were known for their impeccable legal skills, but more so for their ability to spin hilarious tales about their former clients. These lawyers had seen it all, from outrageous courtroom antics to mind-boggling legal defenses. As the drinks flowed, so did the stories, each one more absurd and amusing than the last. This is a collection of their most memorable tales, as told from multiple perspectives.

The Case of the Misplaced Briefs Perspective 1: Alice

Alice was known for her meticulous nature, always prepared and organized. However, she couldn't help but chuckle as she recalled the case of Mr. Thompson, a man accused of stealing a pair of briefs from a high-end department store. Mr. Thompson, in his defense, claimed that the briefs had magically appeared in his shopping bag.Attorney Alice was a confident and skilled lawyer who always delivered results. Her latest client, Mr. Thompson, however, was something of a challenge. He was a bit of a mobile troubleshooter, always on the move, and never quite sure where to go. Alice knew this because Mr. Thompson kept referring her to different places and people to help him with various issues, but nothing seemed to stick.That was until one day when Mr. Thompson walked into Alice's office with a fresh problem on his mind. He had received a letter from his ex-wife, and the contents were troubling. In the letter, she accused him of being mentally unstable and threatening to take legal action against him. Mr. Thompson was at a loss. He had never thought of himself as unstable, and he didn't know what to do. Alice listened to Mr. Thompson's story and immediately recognized the problem. In his haste to move forward, Mr. Thompson had misplaced his briefs, and now he had to find them before his ex-wife could move forward with her claims. Alice knew just the place to look. The next day, Alice took Mr. Thompson to the nearest adult bookstore. They walked around for a while, looking at the various posters on the walls and the various toys on the shelves. They even tried to ask the shopkeeper for help, but he shook his head and left them hanging. After an hour of wandering around, Alice spotted a man in a brightly colored robe walking towards them. He looked like he had just left a waiting room and was on his way out. Alice began to fear that they had blown their cover, but the man seemed to recognize Mr. Thompson, and they followed him outside.The man led them to a small alleyway behind the store, where he pulled out a large basket of briefs. He handed Mr. Thompson a few to try on, and suggested he come back with more. Mr. Thompson was nervous, but he agreed, feeling a little better.Alice stayed close to Mr. Thompson the entire time, making sure that everything went well. When they returned with more briefs, the man showed them to the waiting Mr. Thompson. He tried on one of the briefs, feeling a surge of confidence. The man seemed pleased, and Mr. Thompson thanked him profusely. As they went back to Alice's office, Mr. Thompson was smiling again. He felt relieved and confident that he would be able to find his way through this ex-wife's allegations. Alice could see the change in him, and she was happy to have played a small role in helping. Over the next few days, Alice worked closely with Mr. Thompson to come up with a plan to handle the situation. They went to court, where Mr. Thompson told the judge everything that had happened, including the missing briefs. The judge was skeptical of the ex-wife's claims, and when Mr. Thompson demonstrated that the briefs were missing due to an honest mistake, the judge dismissed the case. The ex-wife was furious, but Mr. Thompson had won. For the first time in months, he felt confident in his own skin. Alice had facilitated a solution that had brought peace of mind to both parties. As they packed up their things to leave, Mr. Thompson turned to Alice and thanked her again for her help. Alice smiled and patted his shoulder. "Don't thank me, Mr. Thompson. You made all of this Prosecutor Paul, who was assigned to the case, couldn't believe his luck. He had seen some bizarre cases, but this one took the cake. The courtroom erupted in laughter as Mr. Thompson earnestly explained how the briefs appeared out of thin air. Even the judge struggled to maintain a straight face.Paul was known for his quick wit and outrageous courtroom antics. He was the ultimate courtroom comedian, making his opponents and even the judge laugh. He loved to entertain the courtroom with his wit and was often compared to the great Monty Python.Every day in court, Paul would strut into the courtroom, wearing a suit that was two sizes too big, a tie that looked like it was drawn on with a Sharpie, and a confident grin that could light up the entire room. He would take his place on the front row, next to his trusty sidekick, the monkey. The monkey was a little fella with a big fluffy tail, and he would often bark in support of Paul's jokes. The two were inseparable, and they were known to pull pranks happen. You're the one who deserves the recognition." And with that, Mr. Thompson left Alice's office feeling better than he had in a long time. He felt like he could take on anything, thanks to the help of his attorney, Alice. As for Alice, she knew that her job was to help her clients overcome their challenges, and that her success was a reflection of Mr. Thompson's strength and determination. Together, they had made a difference in someone's life, and that was all that mattered.

Perspective 2: Prosecutor Paul

on the judge, who had started to fear the antics of the comedy duo. One day, the case that Paul was representing was a high profile one. The defendant was a well-known CEO, and the case was filled with important testimony. The courtroom was packed, and Paul was nervous. He knew that this day would decide the outcome of the case. As the case progressed, Paul began to feel uneasy. He could feel the weight of the jury's eyes on him, and his heart started to race. The atmosphere in the courtroom was tense, and it seemed like the entire world was watching as he testified. When it came time for Paul to make his closing argument, he took a deep breath and began to speak."Ladies and gentlemen of the jury, this case is about a company called Big Blue. Big Blue is a huge corporation that has claimed the rights to use a certain technology that could revolutionize the world's energy grid. The CEO of Big Blue, Mr. Blake, is a powerful man who has a lot of money and influence. But, there is a problem. Mr. Blake has been lying and cheating his way to the top. His testimony today will show you that he is not worthy of the position of CEO. The truth will come out, and you will see that Mr. Blake is not fit to hold any position of authority." Paul paused, and his eyes bored into the jury box. He could feel the eyes of the judge and the spectators on him. The atmosphere in the courtroom had changed, and the crowd was now biting their tongues, restraining themselves from laughing at the ridiculous claims of the attorney. Paul continued, "But, Mr. Blake's lawyers have done a great job of spinning their narrative. They have convinced you that this case is about nothing more than money and power. They have eroded your faith in the legal system and tricked you into believing that everything is just a game.But, I know better. I know that Mr. Blake's actions have hurt many people, and he should be held accountable for his actions." As Paul finished, there was a collective sigh of relief in the courtroom. The verdict was in Paul's favor, and he had won the case. The whole courtroom was filled with a sense of awe and admiration for the attorney. As Paul and his sidekick made their way out of the courtroom, they were mobbed by jubilant attorneys, reporters, and spectators. The whole courthouse buzzed with excitement, and Paul's antics were the talk of the town. The judge announced that there would be a reception to celebrate the victory, and invited all the participants in the case. Paul and the monkey were dressed in their finest suits, and they made their way to the reception. As they arrived, they were greeted with shouts of "Congratulations!" and "You did it!" They were surrounded by their supporters, and Paul felt a sense of fulfillment and accomplishment. As the night wore on, Paul and the monkey regaled the attendees with their courtroom stories, making the party even more memorable. Paul had left his mark on the legal world and had become a legend. As the night ended, Paul and the monkey made their way back to their car. They looked at each other and smiled."That was one hell of a party," the monkey said, wagging his tail. Paul patted him on the head. "You're right, Buddy. But, we've got a lot more work to do. We've got a lot of people who need our help."And with that, the two fell asleep, dreaming of the legal battles that lay ahead.

The Case of the Talking Parrot Perspective 1: Defense Attorney David

Defense Attorney David had always prided himself on taking on unusual cases, but defending Mr. Peterson, accused of teaching his parrot to slander his neighbors, was a whole new level of eccentricity. The courtroom was filled with laughter as the parrot, aptly named Chatterbox, repeated colorful insults that Mr. Peterson claimed he had never taught him.Paul was known for his quick wit and outrageous courtroom antics. He was the ultimate courtroom comedian, making his opponents and even the judge laugh. He loved to entertain the courtroom with his wit and was often compared to the great Monty Python. Every day in court, Paul would strut into the courtroom, wearing a suit that was two sizes too big, a tie that looked like it was drawn on with a Sharpie, and a confident grin that could light up the entire room. He would take his place on the front row, next to his trusty sidekick, the monkey. The monkey was a little fella with a big fluffy tail, and he would often bark in support of Paul's jokes. The two were inseparable, and they were known to pull pranks on the judge, who had started to fear the antics of the comedy duo. One day, the case that Paul was representing was a high profile one. The defendant was a well-known CEO, and the case was filled with important testimony. The courtroom was packed, and Paul was nervous. He knew that this day would decide the outcome of the case. As the case progressed, Paul began to feel uneasy. He could feel the weight of the jury's eyes on him, and his heart started to race. The atmosphere in the courtroom was tense, and it seemed like the entire world was watching as he testified. When it came time for Paul to make his closing argument, he took a deep breath and began to speak. "Ladies and gentlemen of the jury, this case is about a company called Big Blue. Big Blue is a huge corporation that has claimed the rights to use a certain technology that could revolutionize the world's energy grid. The CEO of Big Blue, Mr. Blake, is a powerful man who has a lot of money and influence. But, there is a problem. Mr. Blake has been lying and cheating his way to the top. His testimony today will show you that he is not worthy of the position of CEO. The truth will come out, and you will see that Mr. Blake is not fit to hold any position of authority." Paul paused, and his eyes bored into the jury box. He could feel the eyes of the judge and the spectators on him. The atmosphere in the courtroom had changed, and the crowd was now biting their tongues, restraining themselves from laughing at the ridiculous claims of the attorney. Paul continued, "But, Mr. Blake's lawyers have done a great job of spinning their narrative. They have convinced you that this case is about nothing more than money and power. They have eroded your faith in the legal system and tricked you into believing that everything is just a game. But, I know better. I know that Mr. Blake's actions have hurt many people, and he should be held accountable for his actions." As Paul finished, there was a collective sigh of relief in the courtroom. The verdict was in Paul's favor, and he had won the case. The whole courtroom was filled with a sense of awe and admiration for the attorney. As Paul and his sidekick made their way out of the courtroom, they were mobbed by jubilant attorneys, reporters, and spectators. The whole courthouse buzzed with excitement, and Paul's antics were the talk of the town. The judge announced that there would be a reception to celebrate the victory, and invited all the participants in the case. Paul and the monkey were dressed in their finest suits, and they made their way to the reception. As they arrived, they were greeted with shouts of "Congratulations!" and "You did it!" They were surrounded by their supporters, and Paul felt a sense of fulfillment and accomplishment. As the night wore on, Paul and the monkey regaled the attendees with their courtroom stories, making the party even more memorable. Paul had left his mark on the legal world and had become a legend. As the night ended, Paul and the monkey made their way back to their car. They looked at each other and smiled. "That was one hell of a party," the monkey said, wagging his tail. Paul patted him on the head. "You're right, Buddy. But, we've got a lot more work to do. We've got a lot of people who need our help." And with that, the two fell asleep, dreaming of the legal battles that lay ahead.

Perspective 2: Judge Jennifer

Judge Jennifer, presiding over the case, couldn't help but find the situation amusing. She struggled to maintain her judicial composure as the parrot continued to unleash a flurry of insults at everyone in the courtroom, including the prosecutor. It was a day she would never forget. "Hello, Ms. Johnson," the defense attorney said, extending his hand. "I am David Thompson, Mr. Peterson's defense attorney." "Nice to meet you," the woman said, offering her hand. "I'm Sarah Johnson. I live across the street from Mr. Peterson." David was a seasoned defense attorney who had defended countless clients accused of all kinds of crimes. As he sat down with Sarah and started discussing the case, he knew he had his work cut out for him. Mr. Peterson was accused of teaching his parrot to slander his neighbors, and thus he was facing a hefty fine or even jail time. But David was determined to defend his client to the best of his ability. He knew that a skillful defense attorney could often help his clients avoid serious charges altogether. The first trial ended in a hung jury, and the second trial ended in a mistrial. David had lost both cases, and Mr. Peterson was now facing a third trial in a month's time. As he sat with Sarah, David couldn't help but feel the tension rising in the room. Mr. Peterson was a rambunctious bird, and his cage in the courtroom caused a lot of commotion. The parrot was hooting and screeching incessantly, and it was clear that it wasn't happy in its little cage. Occasionally, the parrot would perch on David's shoulder and whispered in his ear. David would nod and try to calm the bird, but it was impossible to ignore the hostility in its voice. "I think he's been coached," Sarah said, crossing her arms. "I heard he taught his parrot to slander my husband and his entire neighborhood. He's a terrible man." David knew that Sarah was only trying to protect her own interests, but he couldn't help feeling angry at her comments. The defense was hard enough without people using it as an opportunity to dish out their own personal vendettas.As the trial went on, David had to focus all his energy on defending Mr. Peterson against the slander accusations. He had to debunk the evidence of the parrot's alleged wrongdoing, and he had to show that the bird's testimony was unreliable. It was a long, tough battle, but David managed to prove that the parrot couldn't possibly be the culprit. And finally, after two grueling weeks in court, the judge dismissed the case against Mr. Peterson. The parrot screeched with joy as it flew out of its cage, and David gave it a gentle stroke on its head. The bird seemed relieved and didn't mind sitting on David's shoulder anymore. As they left the courtroom, Sarah smiled at David. "Thank you for fighting for my husband," she said. "I know it wasn't an easy case." "No, it wasn't," David said, feeling proud of himself for having done his best. "But I am glad we finally got to the bottom of this." The parrot chirped in agreement and flew up to the window, peering outside with its big round eyes. David smiled as he watched the bird dance in the sunlight, feeling relieved to have gotten Mr. Peterson off the hook. As he walked out of the courthouse, David knew that defending Mr. Peterson had been a long and grueling battle, but he was proud to have helped the little blue bird fly free once again.

The Case of the Invisible Witness

Perspective 1: Attorney Alex

Attorney Alex was renowned for his ability to win seemingly unwinnable cases. However, the case of Mrs. Johnson, accused of theft, tested even his skills. Mrs. Johnson's defense rested on the testimony of an invisible witness that only she claimed to see.

Attorney Alex's Office

Monday Morning

Alex stood at the front of his office, looking out at the busy street outside. His desk was cluttered with files, notes, and court transcripts, but he barely noticed any of it. His mind was on one thing: the case of the Invisible Witness. It was a baffling case, to say the least. Last week, Alex had accepted a blackmailing request from a client who claimed to have incriminating evidence against her husband. The evidence, the client claimed, was a letter written by the husband, which she had obtained after hiring an invisible witness to spy on him. The catch: the letter could only be read by a special reader, and the reader was invisible. Alex had never heard of such a thing, but he had no other choice but to take the case. The wife, who went by the name of Mrs. Johnson, claimed that her husband had been cheating on her and that the evidence was irrefutable proof. Alex, on the other hand, found little to no evidence to support the wife's claim. He doubted the client's story and wondered if she just wanted money. Despite his doubts, the case intrigued Alex. As a lawyer, he loved to uncover the truth, no matter how dark and twisted it was. He knew that a trial would be long and difficult, but he was determined to prove the client's claims false. Slowly but surely, Alex dug through the records and conducted interviews with the parties involved in the case. He spoke to the invisible witness, who claimed to have seen nothing, and found out that the wife had hired him before. He had testified that the husband was innocent, but the court had found him guilty anyway. With this new evidence, Alex was confident that he could prove that the client had paid an invisible witness to lie. He planned to use the evidence to cast doubt on the client's claims, and then expose her as a liar. After days of careful preparation, Alex was set to cross-examine the invisible witness on Monday morning. He hoped that the witness would reveal the truth, and that the truth would set the client free. As the trial got underway, Alex's hopes were dashed. The witness claimed that he could not see the evidence because it was hidden from sight. Alex asked how he knew it was hidden, but the answer remained elusive. The trial continued for hours, but nothing seemed to progress. The client seemed unphased, even when Alex found out that the wife had paid her sister to spy on her husband. She just laughed it off, saying that her sister was trustworthy. After an exhausting day, Alex looked at the clock and realized that it was already midnight. He decided to call it a day and go home. As he packed up his things and left the office, Alex couldn't help but think about the Invisible Witness case. It was baffling, to say the least, and he couldn't help but wonder if he had done the right thing. But as Alex walked out into the street, he realized that the case was just that - a case. It was nothing more than a mystery he had been tasked to solve. And even if he couldn't solve it, he was proud of himself for trying.

Perspective 2: Court Reporter Rachel

Court Reporter Rachel couldn't believe her ears as Mrs. Johnson passionately argued with an invisible entity on the witness stand. The courtroom erupted in laughter as Mrs. Johnson pleaded with the invisible witness to speak up, causing even the judge to question her sanity. As the lawyers continued sharing their hilarious stories, they realized that amidst the laughter, they had also learned valuable lessons about the absurdity of life and the unpredictable nature of the legal system. These tales had become a reminder that even in the most serious of professions, humor could be found. And so, every Friday night, the lawyers of Jesterfield gathered at "Legally Intoxicated" to celebrate their profession and share their outrageous stories, creating a bond that went beyond the courtroom walls.Rachel worked her dream job as a court reporter for a local newspaper. She loved bringing justice to her community, transcribing everything that happened in court, from arguments to verdicts. It was a stressful job, but Rachel found it cathartic to tell the stories that were often ignored by the general public. One afternoon, Rachel and her colleagues decided to try a new bar downtown. They were looking forward to a fun night out and hoped the food and atmosphere would be up to their standards. The bar was buzzing with lively conversations and laughter as they walked in. As they grabbed a seat at the bar, they saw three men gathered around a table. The men were drinking heavily and appeared to be under the influence of some type of drugs. Rachel and her colleagues were hesitant to approach them, but they couldn't resist getting a closer look. As they got closer, one of the men caught their eye and started speaking to them in a slurred voice. Rachel and her colleagues pulled back, but a group of rowdy patrons immediately surrounding them. The tables were pushed together, and the group pressed in on them.Rachel was a nervous wreck, but she knew she had to stay calm and protect her colleagues. As the situation escalated, the police were called to the scene. They quickly arrived and dealt with the situation.Rachel and her colleagues left the bar and walked down the street, trying to process what had just happened. They decided to go to a nearby coffee shop to relax and gather their thoughts. As the coffee shop filled with the sound of steaming cups and the buzz of conversation, Rachel felt a wave of relief wash over her. She realized that the ordeal had only strengthened her resolve to continue doing what she loved. She was grateful to have such a supportive network of friends and colleagues who would always have each other's backs. Eventually, night fell, and Rachel and her colleagues headed back to their respective homes. Before they knew it, it was morning, and the court would be in session. Rachel grabbed her notebook and headed for the courthouse, feeling more determined than ever to bring justice to the community. As she transcribed the day's proceedings, Rachel felt a deep sense of satisfaction. She knew that she had done her job well, transcribing the story of the day. And as she made her way home, she smiled to herself, knowing that in her line of work, anything could happen, but that her colleagues would always have her back.

Ch.5 The Lawyers Guide To Love

Amidst the chaos of their professional lives, the lawyers also faced personal challenges. Sarah found herself torn between her work and a budding romance with a charismatic opposing counsel. The lawyers' love lives became a source of endless amusement, with disastrous blind dates, awkward encounters, and unexpected surprises. "Lawfully In Love" is a heartwarming and humorous tale of two lawyers who find love amidst the chaos of their legal careers. Through their episodic adventures, Sarah and Daniel prove that love and laughter can conquer all, even in the most unexpected circumstances. In the bustling city of Veridale, the prestigious law firm of Johnson & Associates was renowned for its exceptional legal expertise. The firm's most brilliant attorneys, Emily Anderson and Daniel Roberts, were both highly respected and admired by their colleagues. Emily, a sharp-witted and ambitious lawyer, had recently joined the firm after graduating at the top of her class. Daniel, on the other hand, was a seasoned lawyer known for his quick thinking and charismatic personality. Their paths crossed the day Sarah joined the firm, and sparks flew instantly. As Sarah and Daniel worked together on a high-profile case, their professional relationship began to evolve into something more. Their witty banter and shared passion for justice made them a formidable team in the courtroom. However, their growing feelings for each other presented a dilemma. They were hesitant to jeopardize their careers and the harmony within the firm. Unbeknownst to Sarah and Daniel, their colleagues had noticed the undeniable chemistry between them. Emily, a paralegal with a knack for meddling, decided to take matters into her own hands. With the help of her mischievous friends, she orchestrated a series of "coincidental" encounters, hoping to push the two lawyers closer together. Just as Sarah and Daniel were about to confess their feelings for each other, a misunderstanding occurred. A rival law firm's handsome attorney, Michael, expressed his interest in Sarah, leaving Daniel feeling disheartened and confused. Meanwhile, Sarah was torn between her newfound connection with Daniel and the attention she was receiving from Michael. During an important deposition, Sarah accidentally spilled coffee all over her notes, causing chaos in the courtroom. Daniel, ever the quick thinker, managed to turn the situation into a comical distraction, leaving everyone in stitches. This incident brought Sarah and Daniel closer than ever as they laughed off their mishap, realizing that their connection was too strong to ignore. As Sarah and Daniel continued to navigate their feelings, they found solace in their shared sense of humor. Their colleagues, who had been rooting for them from the beginning, decided to intervene one last time. They organized a surprise office party, where Sarah and Daniel finally confessed their love for each other. With their love out in the open, Sarah and Daniel faced a new challenge: balancing their personal and professional lives. While they were determined to make it work, the unpredictable nature of their jobs often led to hilarious situations. From courtroom antics to office pranks, they navigated the ups and downs of their relationship with laughter and unwavering support from their colleagues.

Ch.6 The Great Escape

In the final chapter, Sarah and her colleagues decided to take a much-needed vacation to a secluded island. However, their plans for a peaceful getaway were soon shattered when they stumbled upon a mysterious treasure map. What followed was a hilarious treasure hunt, complete with booby traps, mistaken identities, and an unexpected twist that left everyone in stitches. Sarah and her colleagues had been looking forward to going on vacation for months. Finally, it was their turn to pick where they would go. They were all graduates of top law schools, with plenty of experience in the courtroom, and they were eager to explore a new location. Their destination was a secluded island, far from both the mainland and the bustling city. The weather was perfect, with clear blue skies and gentle waves lapping against the shore. Sarah and her colleagues booked a rustic cabin on the island, and they spent their first day basking in the sun and the pristine nature of the place. As the day went on, the group decided to explore the island by foot. They set out on the scenic path that lead them to a clearing in the forest. In the center of the clearing stood a statue of a winged horse, the symbol of their destination, the magical island of enchantment. Without warning, a gust of wind blew through the group, lifting Sarah's hair out of her bun and sending her sandal flying off her foot. As she bent down to retrieve her shoe, she heard a rustling sound in the bushes behind her. Without thinking, she stood up, prepared for an attack. Suddenly, a loud screeching noise echoed through the forest, and a group of fairies appeared out of nowhere. They were tiny, with sparkling wings and perfect green skin, but Sarah didn't need to see to believe that they were real. They had attacked the group, and Sarah saw her colleagues falling to the ground one by one, their bodies wracked with pain. Sarah knew she had to act fast. She drew her weapon and charged at the fairies, determined to save her colleagues. She struggled with one of them, and managed to bite him, allowing her to take control of the creature. She used it to distract the others, buying her time to reach her colleagues. Once she had managed to bring the fairies under control, Sarah knew she had to get them to the hospital. She managed to lead them back to their cabin and made the creatures an offer they couldn't refuse. She offered to take them to the mainland and turn them over to the authorities if they would help her find the most urgent medical attention. With her newfound allies at her side, Sarah and her colleagues made it to the medical center just in time. They were rushed into surgery and were miraculously okay, with only a few minor cuts and scratches. Afterwards, Sarah thanked the fairies for their help. They told her that they had only attacked the group because they were under orders from an evil wizard who had been trying to take the island for himself. They warned her and her colleagues about the danger of the island and urged them to find an alternate way to explore it. As they boarded the ferry back to the mainland, Sarah felt a sense of awe and wonder in being part of such an incredible adventure. She knew that she would never forget her time on the enchanted island, and that she would always remember the magic and wonder of the magical world she had discovered.

Ch. 7 The Laughter Continues

"Sarah sat at her desk, surrounded by her colleagues in the bustling office of Summers Associate. They were a team of quirky individuals, each with their own unique personality and absurd stories to share. Sarah, a witty and quick-thinking woman, had a knack for turning the most mundane client stories into hilarious anecdotes."Okay, guys, gather around," Sarah exclaimed, waving her arms to get everyone's attention. "I've got a client story that will have you rolling on the floor laughing!" Her colleagues, a mixture of equally eccentric individuals, gathered eagerly around her desk. There was Mark, the tech geek with a penchant for puns, Lisa, the fashionista who always had a story to tell, and Peter, the office prankster who loved stirring up mischief. Sarah began, "So, I had this client, Mrs. Jenkins, who came in complaining about her new set of dentures. Apparently, they had a mind of their own!" The room erupted in laughter, and Sarah continued, her eyes sparkling with mischief. "She told me that one night, as she was getting ready for bed, she took out her dentures and placed them on the nightstand. But the next morning, she woke up to find them dancing on the kitchen table!"The team burst into fits of laughter, picturing the absurd image in their minds. Mark chimed in, "Maybe they were practicing for a talent show!"Lisa, snorting with laughter, added, "Can you imagine dentures doing the cha-

cha? That's a sight I'd pay to see!" Peter, unable to contain himself, interjected, "Maybe they were just trying to escape her mouth! I mean, who wouldn't want to run away from Mrs. Jenkins' bad breath?"The room erupted in laughter once again, and Sarah wiped away tears of mirth. "Oh, you guys! But wait, it gets even better. Mrs. Jenkins was convinced her dentures were possessed!"The team leaned in closer, their eyes wide with anticipation. Sarah continued, "She said that every night, she would hear faint whispers coming from her dentures, as if they were plotting something. She even caught them watching late-night TV when she thought she had turned them off!"The team burst into uncontrollable laughter, tears streaming down their faces. Sarah's storytelling prowess had turned a simple client complaint into a hilarious comedy sketch.As the laughter subsided, Sarah looked around at her colleagues, each wearing a wide grin. "I love working with you guys. We turn even the most mundane stories into comedy gold!"Day by Day, Sarah and her colleagues continued to regale each other with outrageous client stories, transforming the office into a never-ending comedy show. From the absurd to the downright bizarre, they found humor in every situation, making their workdays a little brighter.And so, the hilarious chronicles of Sarah and Summers Associates. continued, bringing laughter and joy to all who crossed their path. With their dialogue-driven storytelling style and unwavering camaraderie, they turned the ordinary into the extraordinary, one client story at a time.

Epilogue Life Goes On

In the end, Sarah and her fellow lawyers realized that laughter was the best remedy for the pressures of their profession. Their tell-all book became a bestseller, bringing joy and laughter to readers around the world. As they continued their legal careers, they never forgot the importance of finding humor in the most unexpected places.